FISK UNIVERSITY LIBRARY

D1066063

The Stolen Ruler

The Stolen Ruler

by

Eric W. Johnson

Illustrated by June Goldsborough

J. B. LIPPINCOTT COMPANY
Philadelphia   New York

To Claude Nell,
once an eighth grader on St. Croix,
whose experience is the basis
for this story.

Text Copyright © 1970 by Eric W. Johnson
Illustrations Copyright © 1970 by June Goldsborough
ALL RIGHTS RESERVED
Printed in the United States of America
Library of Congress Catalog Card Number: 72-117239
FIRST EDITION

Contents

The
Stolen
Ruler

Chapter 1

How Claude Got the Ruler

Claude Sample was six. He lived with his mother and father in two rooms of a row house in a small city. His father was a carpenter.

One evening after supper Mrs. Sample was washing the dishes, and Claude was lying on the floor looking at a book, almost reading it. His father looked at him and said, "Hey, Claude."

"Yeah, Pop?" said Claude.

His father was holding a stick in his hand. "Son," he said, "shall I show you how to tell how long things are?"

"Sure, Pop," said Claude. He always liked it when his dad took time to teach him something.

"Well, Claude," said Dad, "look at this stick. What is it called?"

"A ruler," said Claude. "I know that. You use it to measure things."

"That's right. Now look at it closely. Do you see these numbers? What do you think they are?"

"I know!" said Claude, feeling very bright. "They're 1, 2, 3, 4, 5, 6, 7, 8, 9, 10, 11, 12." He pointed at each number as he counted.

"Great," said his dad. "And each number marks off one space and each space is called one inch."

"One inch," repeated Claude. "So there are twelve inches on the ruler, right?"

"Right! You're bright," his dad said, smiling. "In fact, you're so bright I'm going to give you something."

"What?" asked Claude. Then he saw his father was taking a long, narrow package out of his toolbox.

"Here," said Dad, "open this."

Claude untied the string. Then he unrolled the paper, and he saw that the package was a bag. He reached into the bag. In the bottom was a ruler.

"Gee!" said Claude. "That's neat!" He looked at the ruler closely. It was made of smooth wood. Claude could see the grain. It was shiny with varnish. It had numbers on it just like Dad's ruler. It also had yellow metal along one edge, the same edge that had the numbers.

"1, 2, 3, 4, 5, 6, 7, 8, 9, 10, 11, 12," said Claude.

"Twelve what?" asked Dad.

"Twelve inches," said Claude. "You already told me that."

"O.K.," said Dad. "I just wanted to see if you remembered. Now see if you can use your ruler to measure something. How long is this book?"

Claude put his ruler against the book and counted up the inches: "1, 2, 3, 4, 5, 6, 7, 8, and—and a little bit," he said.

"Right as usual!" said his dad. "Now I'll show you how to tell how long the little bit is."

"O.K.," said Claude.

"Look closely. See how in each inch there are some lines?"

"Yeah," said Claude.

"How many lines are there in each inch?" asked Dad.

Claude counted. "Three," he said.

"And how many spaces in each inch?" asked Dad.

Claude counted again. "Four spaces," he said.

"Right as usual!" said Dad. "And each space is called a quarter of an inch. So how many quarters of an inch are there in each inch?"

"Four!" said Claude. "That's easy."

"O.K., so how long is that book?" Dad asked.

Claude measured the book again. "Eight inches and one quarter," said Claude.

Claude's dad smiled again. "You are so right. Only you call it eight and a quarter inches."

"Right!" said Claude, sounding just like his father.

"O.K.," said Dad. "Now, that's your ruler. Take care of it."

"But it's not even my birthday," said Claude.

"I know it's not. I just thought you might like to have a ruler. See what you can measure with it," said Dad, and he gave Claude a light tap on the seat with his own ruler, as Claude ran out of the kitchen and into the bedroom to start measuring. He almost ran into Mrs. Sample, who said, "Claude, it's time to go to bed."

"Aw, Mom!" said Claude, but he went.

Chapter 2

Claude Measures Things

The next day was Saturday, so there wasn't any school. Claude woke up early, but he didn't open his eyes. He just listened and he heard his mother and father breathing in their sleep on the other side of the room. Eyes still closed, he reached out to the table beside his bed to feel whether his ruler was where he had put it last night. He felt it, all right. Without looking, he felt all over the ruler—the metal edge, the smooth, varnished wood, the little dents where the numbers and lines were. He even tried to feel each number, 1 through 12, but that wasn't easy.

Then he got up very quietly and tiptoed into the kitchen, closing the door softly. He took the ruler with him.

"Now I'm going to measure things," he said to himself. First he measured that book again. It was still eight

and a quarter inches long. Then he measured a spoon. It was six and a quarter inches long. Then he measured a fork and a knife, and they were seven and two quarters inches long and eight and two quarters inches long.

He heard a quiet thump. Fred, the cat, had dropped off a chair onto the floor. Fred lay down on a small rug in front of the sink. He curled his tail around his back legs and up toward his front feet. The tail looked good for measuring. So Claude took the end of Fred's tail and held it straight. Then he put the ruler down beside the tail. He started to count the inches, but slowly the tail curled up again. When Claude tried to hold it straight, Fred said, "Rowlll!" and put out his claws.

"Oh, well," thought Claude. "I guess I can only measure straight things. You'd need three hands to measure Fred's tail." So he measured his foot, from the heel to the end of his big toe. It was just six inches long.

Then Claude yawned and looked at himself in a long mirror by the door. His mouth looked big, yawning. "I'll measure my mouth, wide open," he thought. "Mom always says it's too big." So he opened his mouth wide and put one end of the ruler against his top teeth. Then he marked with his finger where the bottom teeth came on the ruler. When he looked at the ruler, he was surprised. His mouth, wide open, measured only one and and two quarters inches wide.

He opened his mouth again, so wide that it ached, and put the ruler against his top teeth.

"What in the world are you doing, Claude?" said his mother's voice behind him. She was laughing.

"I'm measuring my mouth," said Claude. He felt a little silly.

"Don't worry, Claude. It's big enough. Both for putting things into and for talking words out of."

"It's not so big, Mom. It's only one and two quarters inches big, wide open," said Claude.

"That's one and a half inches, and that's plenty of mouth for a six-year-old," said his mother. "Now you get washed and dressed."

Chapter 3

Marking the Ruler

On Sunday afternoon Claude was playing on the steps outside the house with his friend Otis Link. They were playing with some sticks, pretending they were cars.

"Brrrrrm!" said Claude, pushing his stick up the side of the steps.

"Screeeeeech!" said Otis, stopping his stick suddenly so that it wouldn't run into Claude's.

"Hey!" said Claude suddenly. "I just remembered. Tomorrow is Monday. School!"

"Yeah," said Otis, "another day of first grade."

"You know," said Claude, "I'm going to take my new ruler to school. There might be something that needs measuring."

"I dunno," said Otis. "Old Mrs. Clipper might not like it. Maybe you're not supposed to have a ruler."

That made Claude a little bit angry. "Not supposed to? I can take a ruler to school if I want to. It's a free country!" said Claude. He often heard his father say "It's a free country," and he thought it sounded good.

"Maybe it's a free country," said Otis, "but it's not a free school."

"Well, I'm going to take the ruler," said Claude. "Hey, Otis, want to see my ruler?" Before Otis could answer, Claude popped into the house and popped out again. "Here!" he said, his eyes shining.

"That's neat," said Otis. "But if you're going to take it to school, you'd better put your name on it."

"That's a good idea," said Claude. He already knew how to write his name, but that was about all he could write. "You hold the ruler, Otis; I'll get a pencil."

When Claude came back with a pencil, Otis was studying the ruler. "Gimme it," said Claude. Then he put the ruler down on the step and tried to write a C, but the pencil just slipped and slid on the shiny varnish and hard wood.

"It won't write," said Claude. "It's too slippery." It was true. The pencil point just slipped around and made hardly any mark at all. And when Claude rubbed the light marks hard with his thumb, they rubbed right off.

"Well, that won't work," said Otis, who had been watching closely. "Now what are you going to do?"

Claude thought. "Hey!" he said. "Otis, have you got your knife?"

"Sure," said Otis. "I always have it in case of emergencies."

"Well, this is an emergency. Gimme it," said Claude, and then he added, "please," because he remembered how much Otis loved his knife.

"O.K.," said Otis. He handed over the knife. "Now what are you going to do?"

"I'm going to carve some special marks," said Claude. As Otis watched, Claude carefully cut four little notches in one end of the ruler, the end that had "12" on it. Four little V-shaped pieces of wood fell on the step. "There!" said Claude. "Now I'll know it's my ruler in case anything happens."

"Neat," said Otis. He looked at the "12" end closely. "Four notches. A little, a little, a big, and a little."

"A little, a little, a big, and a little," said Claude.

But Otis was thinking. Then he said, "But notches aren't a name. Suppose—" Just then he heard a shout down the street.

"Otis, boy, you come home, but *now!*" It was his mother, and when she yelled that way, you'd better come quick.

"I gotta go, so long!" said Otis, and ran down the street before Claude could find out what he was supposing.

Claude looked at his ruler. He rubbed his finger over the notches. "Neat!" he said to himself. "A little, a little, a big, and a little." He knew that nobody could ever have a ruler with four notches just like his four notches.

Chapter 4

Claude Takes the Ruler to School

Next morning, Claude walked into the Nell Elementary School with Otis. It was a small, old school, and almost everything in it was dark and ugly. The boys made their way together down the noisy hall to Room 14, Mrs. Clipper's first grade room.

"I've got it." said Claude. "In my schoolbag."

"Got what?" asked Otis.

"The ruler," said Claude.

"Well, don't leave it lying around," said Otis. "Somebody might like to have a nice new ruler. Especially Roger Beam."

Claude didn't have time to say, "What do you mean, especially Roger Beam?" because they were at the door of Room 14, and you weren't allowed to talk in or even near Mrs. Clipper's room unless Mrs. Clipper said so.

In the morning you were supposed to go to your seat, get a book and look at it, or just sit quietly.

In Room 14, there were six rows, and each row had seven desks and seats. The seats were attached to the desks and the desks were screwed to the floor, so all forty-two places were always in exactly the same place.

"Especially Roger Beam," Claude thought. Roger was the boy who sat just in front of Claude. He was big and he didn't have any friends, and he liked to borrow things. Often when Roger borrowed a thing it never came back. And you were kind of afraid to ask for it back because Roger was big and he had hard fists.

But Roger was always very polite to teachers, especially to Mrs. Clipper.

Claude sat down in his seat, the last one in the second row. Roger's was empty; he hadn't come yet. Claude took out a book to look at. And he quietly opened his schoolbag and took out his ruler. He rubbed his finger over the four notches.

"Mine!" he murmured.

Then he quietly measured the book he was looking at. "Nine and two quarters—I mean nine and a half—inches," he whispered to himself.

The seat in front of Claude creaked. It was Roger sitting down. The room was quiet. The bell to start school had not rung yet. Mrs. Clipper was sitting at her desk in front making marks in a notebook. Claude thought she looked hard and cold. She was a teacher you never argued with.

Just then Roger turned halfway around in his seat. "Hey, Claudie, what have you got there?" he asked.

"It's just a—" Claude started to whisper when Mrs. Clipper said clearly, "Roger, face front, please!"

"O.K., Mrs. Clipper," said Roger. "Claude was just showing me his—"

"That will do, Roger. Claude, you know the rules."

"But—" Claude started to say, but the bell rang, and Mrs. Clipper, with a small frown for Claude, stood up and started the lesson.

Roger's hand went up.

"Yes, Roger?" said Mrs. Clipper.

"Can I pass out the paper, Mrs. Clipper?"

"*May* I pass out the paper," said Mrs. Clipper. "Yes, Roger, that would be very helpful." Mrs. Clipper smiled a small, cold smile, and Roger went forward to be helpful.

Chapter 5

Claude
Loses
the Ruler

It seemed a long time till mid-morning recess. At last the bell rang and Mrs. Clipper said, "You are excused, class. Go quietly."

Claude couldn't wait to get outside and run. He went with Otis and they joined in a game of tag. Too soon, the bell rang and they walked as slowly as possible back to Room 14.

Suddenly Claude remembered something. He said to Otis, "Gee, I forgot. I left my ruler lying beside my book right on my desk!"

"That was dumb," said Otis. "And you didn't see Roger out at recess, did you?"

When Claude got to his desk, there was his book, just where he had left it, but no ruler. Roger didn't look up as Claude sat down. Claude felt sure that Roger had taken his ruler. He wanted to go up and tell Mrs. Clipper but how could he make her believe it? After all, he hadn't seen Roger take it. He didn't know; he only thought.

Mrs. Clipper was writing letters on the board, large, clear letters in yellow chalk. Claude watched her: a, d, s, t, e, o, r, b, x, she wrote. Claude knew all the letters.

"This will be easy," he thought.

Mrs. Clipper smiled her small smile and said, "I need two children, one to point to the letters, one to read what they are. Who would like to volunteer?"

Claude raised his hand. So did Roger. So did most of the other first graders. A few shouted, "Me! Me!"

"I cannot call on you if you shout out," said Mrs. Clipper firmly. "All right, let's see. We'll have Alice and Roger."

Roger got up from his seat. As he did, he knocked a notebook on his desk so that it moved a little. Claude saw that under the notebook, now no longer hidden, was a ruler—his ruler.

"I'm going to get that ruler back," Claude thought. "I don't care what happens." So he waited for his chance.

It was not long in coming. Alice was pointing out the letters, and Roger was saying them, and Mrs. Clipper was looking at them, not at the class. She was saying, "Good, Roger." Claude carefully leaned forward over his desk and quickly pulled the ruler out from under the notebook. He put it quietly on his own desk and covered it with his own notebook.

By the time Mrs. Clipper had said, "Good, Roger,"

for the last time, Claude had his ruler. He had run his finger over the end and felt the four notches. "Mine!" he thought. "Mine!" he knew.

Claude was happy when Roger came back to his seat. He saw him sneak a look under his notebook. He saw him start to turn around to look at Claude, but Mrs. Clipper said, just then, "Heads front, class!" and all heads faced front.

"Now, class, get out your workbooks. Open to Page 7, this page." She held up the book. It was a page covered with large, neat letters. "Copy the letters," she said. "Copy them on your piece of paper. Make straight lines!"

Straight lines. Claude thought of his ruler and its straight, yellow metal edge. "I'll make the straightest lines in the class," he thought.

"Work quietly," Mrs. Clipper was saying. "If you have trouble, come to my desk."

Claude got out his ruler and went to work. He was having fun. His letters were neat, his lines were straight. He heard Roger's seat creak, but he paid no attention. A moment later he glanced up and saw Roger, as usual, politely talking with Mrs. Clipper. "I wonder what his problem is," he thought. Then he went back to his letters and lines and did not notice anything else.

Suddenly, he felt his ruler snatched from his hand. He looked up in anger. Mrs. Clipper stood tall above him, holding the ruler. She was angry.

"Claude, you stole Roger's ruler. You are a thief! You are a thief!" And then she picked up Claude's hand firmly in hers and hit his knuckles hard with the ruler—with his own ruler.

Tears sprang into Claude's eyes. "That's my ruler!" he shouted. He had never shouted in Mrs. Clipper's room before. The whole class was looking at him now.

"Oh, it is, is it?" shouted Mrs. Clipper. She turned to Roger. "Roger, tell the class what you just told me."

"Well," said Roger, "I was up at the board saying those letters . . ."

"Yes, Roger," said Mrs. Clipper.

"Well, I left my ruler under my notebook on my desk. It was a brand-new ruler, the same ruler Mrs. Clipper has in her hand right now."

"But, Mrs. Clipper, it's not his—" Claude interrupted.

"Quiet! Let Roger finish," said Mrs. Clipper. "Go ahead, Roger."

"I got back to my desk and the ruler wasn't there," Roger continued. "Then I looked around while Claude was doing his letters, and he was using *my* ruler. So I went up and told you Claude had my ruler. And so you took it away from him."

While Roger was saying this, Claude was looking at him and hating him. He was so angry he was almost crying. He felt his knuckles aching where they had been hit with his own ruler. But he felt his hate even stronger than the ache. "But it's *my* ruler!" he shouted again. "I can prove it. Just look—"

"Claude, that's enough!" said Mrs. Clipper. "The ruler has Roger's name written on the back very plainly. See, class?" and she held up the ruler. There on the back Claude could see, written in blue Magic Marker, ROGER BEAM.

Claude was amazed. He had not looked at the back of the ruler. But he knew it was his ruler, even if it did have Roger's name on it. He shouted, "But it's *my* ruler. I can prove—"

Mrs. Clipper caught Claude's hand and squeezed it very hard, saying, "Quiet, Claude! If you say one more word, I'll send you to the principal."

"ONE MORE WORD!" shouted Claude. He was amazed at himself. He had sassed a teacher. He had sassed Mrs. Clipper. Then he realized that he really wanted to go to the principal. He'd tell Mr. Trencher the truth.

For a moment Mrs. Clipper looked amazed. Her mouth opened and then shut. The class giggled for a brief moment. Then everything was quiet.

Mrs. Clipper walked slowly and stiffly to her desk and sat down. She looked at Claude fiercely, but suddenly Claude wasn't afraid. His heart was beating very fast, but he wasn't afraid. He knew he was right.

"Did I hear you correctly, Claude?" asked Mrs. Clipper. "What did you say?"

"One more word," said Claude clearly; "that's what I said."

"I thought so," said Mrs. Clipper. "All right, Claude, come and stand by my desk." Claude did as he was told. Mrs. Clipper got out a sheet of paper and started writing a note. Her lips were pressed hard together. Her back was straight. Now and then she looked up at the class, and at Claude, who stood silently by her desk.

"There!" she said. She carefully folded the note and clipped it closed with a paper clip. On the outside she wrote, "Mr. Trencher."

"All right," said Mrs. Clipper. "We'll see what Mr. Trencher does about a thief. Take this at once to the office, Claude. And I am surprised at the way you have behaved."

Then she turned to Roger. "Here, Roger, come and take your ruler back. And, Claude, go!"

Claude took the note and left the classroom. As he closed the door, he heard Mrs. Clipper say, "All right, I hope Claude will learn—" but he didn't hear what Mrs. Clipper hoped he would learn.

He felt rather small walking alone down the big hall toward the principal's office, but he knew he was right.

Chapter 6

Claude Talks to the Principal

Claude went in the doorway of the principal's office and walked up to the counter. He was just tall enough to see over it, and he saw a pretty young secretary sitting at a typewriter. The keys clicked quickly. It seemed a long time before she looked up and saw Claude's head.

"Yes?" she said, smiling.

"I'm supposed to give this note to Mr. Trencher. It's from Mrs. Clipper. She's my teacher." Claude stopped. The secretary looked friendly, so Claude went on. "Mrs. Clipper says I'm a thief, but I'm not a thief."

"Oh?" said the secretary. "Well, you don't look like a thief. What's your name?"

"Claude Sample," said Claude.

"O.K.," said the secretary. "Now, what did you steal?"

"What I did *not* steal is a ruler," said Claude. "It's my ruler."

"Oh," said the secretary. "Well, give me the note, and I'll take it to Mr. Trencher."

Claude gave her the note.

"And don't worry," said the secretary. "Mr. Trencher is a strict man. He is also a fair man. If you did not steal a ruler, Mr. Trencher will find out." She pointed to a chair. "Why don't you sit over there and wait."

Claude waited. The secretary had gone into Mr. Trencher's office and closed the door. Behind the door he heard the principal's voice rumbling. Once he thought he heard it laugh. Then the door opened and the secretary said, "All right, Claude, Mr. Trencher wants to see you. Come on in."

Claude went in. It was the first time he had ever been in the principal's office, but he didn't notice anything but a large, flat desk and Mr. Trencher sitting behind it. Mr. Trencher pointed to a chair and Claude sat down. Then he spoke in a rather loud and rumbly voice.

"Claude," he said, "my secretary tells me you say you are not a thief. Mrs. Clipper's note says you are a thief. Who is right?"

The question came so loudly and so suddenly that Claude couldn't make his voice answer at once.

"Claude," said Mr. Trencher, "do you know what a thief is?"

"Yes," said Claude, "it's somebody who steals something."

"Correct," said Mr. Trencher. "So who is right, Mrs. Clipper or you?"

"I am right because I didn't steal anything. I just took *my* ruler back."

"But Mrs. Clipper's note says it had Roger Beam's name on it," said Mr. Trencher.

"Yes, but I know it is mine," said Claude. "Roger took it."

"Did you see him take it?" asked Mr. Trencher.

"No, but he had it on his desk when I came in from recess," said Claude.

"Can you prove it is your ruler?" asked Mr. Trencher. "I mean, can you tell why anybody would *know*—not just think—it is yours?"

"Sure," said Claude. "I know because when I got the ruler, I borrowed Otis Link's knife, and I—"

"Wait," said Mr. Trencher. "You say you can prove it. All right, I'll give you a chance to prove it, but I haven't got time now to hear all this. But tomorrow morning I will make time, and I'll find out the truth."

"O.K.," said Claude, "because I'm telling the truth."

"We'll see," said Mr. Trencher. "Have you got any evidence?"

"I don't know what ev—ev—"

"Evidence," said Mr. Trencher.

"Evidence," said Claude. "I don't know what evidence is."

"Evidence is something that shows what is really true. It is something you can *see*; it is something you can *feel*; it is something you can *hear*. You need evidence to prove you are right," said Mr. Trencher. Then he pushed a button on his desk and almost at once the secretary came in.

"Yes, Mr. Trencher?" she said.

"Miss Bell, I'd like you to set up a meeting for tomorrow morning in my office here, let's say for second period—9:42. I'd like Mrs. Clipper to be here."

"Mrs. Clipper," repeated Miss Bell. "I'll get a teacher to cover her class for that period."

"Fine," said Mr. Trencher. "And Claude, and either Mr. or Mrs. Sample. We ought to have one of his parents, since he may be in trouble."

"All right," said Miss Bell. "I'll telephone the Samples." She looked at Claude. "Have you got a telephone?"

"Yes, we have," said Claude. "The number is TR4–9672."

"And Roger Beam," said Mr. Trencher.

"Roger Beam," said Miss Bell.

"And—whose knife did you say you borrowed, Claude?" asked Mr. Trencher.

"Otis Link's," said Claude.

"And Otis Link," said Mr. Trencher. "Is he in Mrs. Clipper's room?"

"Yes," said Claude.

"And Otis Link," repeated Miss Bell.

"Fine!" said Mr. Trencher. "I guess that's all." He paused. "Oh, no. One more thing we'll need at the meeting—the ruler. I'll just go down now to Mrs. Clipper's room and get it. I'll keep it here in my office until the meeting. We wouldn't want anything to happen to such an important piece of evidence." He turned to Claude. "All right, Claude, I'll see you to-morrow."

"With evidence," said Claude.

Chapter 7

Claude Looks for Evidence

When Claude got home that afternoon, he was glad to find his mother and father there. They were sitting in the kitchen talking.

"Dad!" said Claude. "I lost my ruler!"

"So I heard, Claude," said his dad.

"How did you hear?" asked Claude, surprised.

"Well, Claude," said his mother, "Mr. Trencher's secretary called."

"Oh, that's right, I forgot," said Claude. "I gave Miss Bell our telephone number."

"Yes, Claude, she called," said Mrs. Sample. "She told me that Mrs. Clipper says you stole a ruler. Mrs. Clipper thinks you are a thief. Mr. Trencher wants your dad or me at school tomorrow at 9:42 to talk about the matter. Say, Claude, what is this?"

"Yes, Claude," said his father, "what's going on? How could you have taken your own ruler? Or did you lose it?"

"It's a pretty long story," said Claude. "Can I have a glass of milk and a cookie first?"

"Sure, Son," said his mother.

And so Claude drank his milk and ate his cookie and told the whole long story. At the end he said, "So you see, I did take the ruler, and Mrs. Clipper thinks it's Roger's because his name is on it, and I didn't have a chance to tell anybody about those four notches we cut in the end."

"Notches?" asked his father. "Who cut notches in the end?"

"Me and Otis," said Claude.

Just then the door opened and Otis came in. "Hi, everybody!" he said.

"Hi, Otis," said Claude and his parents.

"Gee, Claude," said Otis without even asking for a cookie, "that Mrs. Clipper, she's a gyp. That looked like your ruler to me. Wasn't it?"

Before Claude could answer, his father said, "Say, Otis, tell me about those notches."

"A little, a little, a big, and a little," said Otis.

"That's right," said Claude, "a little, a little, a big, and a little."

"Wait a minute," said Claude's father. "I'm lost. What do you mean? You explain, Otis."

"Well," said Otis, "Claude couldn't write his name on the ruler because the pencil kept slipping off, so he borrowed my knife and he cut notches—four notches—in the end."

"In the '12' end," said Claude.

"In the '12' end," said Otis, "and they were a little notch, a little notch, and big notch, and a little."

"Yeah," said Claude, "and that's how I *know* it's my ruler. Because I felt the notches when I took it back from Roger."

"*You* know it's your ruler. *You* know you cut the notches here at home," said Mrs. Sample. "But how does anybody else know? Suppose Roger Beam says you cut them at school *after* you took the ruler back?"

"Hmmm!" said Claude.

"Hey!" said Otis. "Me! I know he cut them. I saw him do it right out on the steps."

"Well, that would help," said Mr. Sample, "but Mrs. Clipper might think Claude just got you to make up

the story about the notches. After all, you're friends. You're always together."

"Hey, wait a minute," Claude said. "When we cut those notches—" he looked at Otis—"four little pieces of wood fell out onto the steps. Maybe they're still there. Mom, you didn't sweep the steps this morning, did you?"

"I'm afraid not. I should have, but I was too busy. Maybe you're lucky," said Mrs. Sample.

"O.K.," said Claude, "if we can find the four pieces, wouldn't that be ev—ev—ev—"

"Evidence?" Claude's father said.

"Yes, evidence! That's what Mr. Trencher wants," said Claude. "Let's go look."

So all four went out on the steps and looked. Claude and Otis got down on their hands and knees and looked very hard and very close.

"Here!" Otis, and he held up a little, V-shaped piece of wood.

"That's one of them," said Claude. "Great! Let's find the others."

In a moment they had found the four pieces—a little, a little, a big, and a little.

"Good," said Claude's mother. "Now, here is an envelope. Put them in it and keep them carefully."

Claude dropped the four precious pieces into the envelope, and Mr. Sample took out a pencil and started writing on the envelope.

"What are you writing, Dad?" asked Claude.

"I'll read it," said Mr. Sample. "I wrote: 'These four bits of wood found on step outside Samples' house on Monday afternoon. Found by Claude Sample, Otis Link, and Mr. and Mrs. Sample.'"

"Boy!" said Claude. "That's real evidence, isn't it?"

Chapter 8

The Meeting in Mr. Trencher's Office

Next morning, Claude woke early. He carefully felt for the envelope in his schoolbag. It was there.

Claude wanted to get to school. He felt a little scared, and a little excited. As he went out the door he waved to his parents. "I'll see you at school, Pop!" he said. "Boy, I can't wait for that first period to be over."

"O.K., Son—at 9:42," said his father.

Claude met Otis and they walked to school together. When they reached Room 14, things were as quiet as usual. Mrs. Clipper was seated stiffly at her desk, and she didn't look up as they came in. Roger Beam was already in his seat. He did look up, and Claude expected him to whisper, "Thief!" or something, but he didn't say anything.

"Gee," thought Claude, "he looks scared." He almost felt sorry for Roger. After all, Roger was a thief, and

Roger didn't have any friends, except Mrs. Clipper. And who wanted Mrs. Clipper for a friend!

The bell rang.

"All right, class," said Mrs. Clipper. "I have an announcement. When the 9:42 bell rings, I have been asked to go to Mr. Trencher's office. You will have another teacher for that period. See that you behave yourselves."

She looked at the class, and the class looked silently at her. "And," continued Mrs. Clipper, "three children are to come with me. Roger Beam." She smiled a little. "Otis Link." She stopped smiling. "And Claude Sample." She frowned a little, and paused.

Claude looked at her. "Gee," he thought, "she looks a little scared, too!" He had never thought that a strict teacher like Mrs. Clipper could be scared.

"All I can say," said Mrs. Clipper, "is that *some* people make a lot of trouble," and she looked, just for an instant, at Claude.

"All right, class, take out your workbooks. . . ." and the lesson began.

At 9:42 the bell rang. The substitute teacher came in, and Mrs. Clipper said, "Good morning, Miss Singer. They are a well-behaved class—most of them. Come with me, Roger and Otis and Claude."

Claude picked up his schoolbag.

"You will not need to take your schoolbag, Claude," said Mrs. Clipper. "It will be perfectly safe here."

"But I will need it," said Claude.

"Well, all right, but it will probably be in the way," said Mrs. Clipper.

They all filed out the door and walked silently down the hall, Mrs. Clipper in the lead. When they reached the counter outside Mr. Trencher's office, Miss Bell was there, smiling. The office door was closed.

"Good morning," said Miss Bell. She turned to Claude. "Claude, your father hasn't arrived yet, so why don't all of you wait a moment—"

Just then Claude heard his father's footsteps coming down the hall. "Here he comes," said Claude, as his father entered.

"Mr. Sample?" asked Miss Bell, turning toward him.

"Yes," said Claude's father. "And you're Miss Bell?"

"That's right," she said. "Good morning. Well, I think everybody's here now." She knocked on Mr. Trencher's door.

"Come in," rumbled the voice inside.

Miss Bell opened the door. "Go right in," she said.

Mrs. Clipper went in first, the boys followed, and Claude's father went in last. They all said, "Good morning, Mr. Trencher." They sat in a half circle in

front of the principal's desk: Mrs. Clipper, Roger, Otis, Claude, and Mr. Sample.

"Well, we might as well start," said Mr. Trencher. "I called this meeting because something has happened. One of our pupils—" he looked at Claude— "has been called a thief by one of our teachers," and he looked at Mrs. Clipper.

"Well, as far as I can tell," said Mrs. Clipper, and she sounded much smaller in the principal's office than she sounded in Room 14.

"She *is* scared!" thought Claude. He looked at Otis, but Otis was looking at Mr. Trencher. He looked at Roger. Roger was looking at his hands and twisting a button on his shirt.

"Mrs. Clipper," said Mr. Trencher, "may I read your note?"

"Certainly," said Mrs. Clipper.

"Fine," said Mr. Trencher. "Mrs. Clipper wrote: 'Claude Sample took Roger Beam's ruler. Roger's name was on the ruler. Claude was rude to me and shouted in class. I cannot have such behavior. I am sending him to you. He needs to be taught a lesson. There's too much stealing in this school.' That's what the note says."

Mr. Trencher looked around. No one spoke. Claude felt like saying, "But it was *my* ruler," but he decided to be quiet. He was glad he did because Mr. Trencher looked at him and asked, "Claude, did you steal Roger's ruler?"

"No, I didn't," said Claude.

Mr. Trencher looked at Roger. "Did Claude take your ruler, Roger?" he said.

"Yes, he did, right off my desk. And my name was on it," said Roger.

"All right," said Mr. Trencher after a pause, "let's see if we can discover what really happened." Mr. Trencher reached into his desk drawer, took out the ruler, and held it up. "Here's the ruler. The question is, whose ruler is it?"

Mr. Trencher paused again. Then he looked at Roger. "Roger, this is your ruler, is it?"

"Yes, it is," said Roger.

"Where did you get it, Roger?" asked Mr. Trencher.

Roger hesitated. "Well—uh, I bought it at a store. And then I put my name on it, so I could know it was mine."

"Did anybody but you know you had the ruler, Roger?" asked Mr. Trencher.

"No, nobody—except Mrs. Clipper, when I told her Claude had stolen it," said Roger.

"How do you know Claude stole it?" asked Mr. Trencher.

"Well, I don't know if I remember everything," said Roger. "But yesterday I had my ruler on my desk. And I went away from my desk, or something, and when I came back—"

"Just a minute, Roger!" It was Mrs. Clipper interrupting. "May I tell exactly what happened, Mr. Trencher?"

"Please do," said Mr. Trencher.

"We were having a letter-reading lesson," said Mrs. Clipper. "Alice Kurtz and Roger were pointing and reading letters I had written on the board. We were looking at the board. I did not see what was going on behind my back." She looked at Claude.

"Then," Mrs. Clipper went on, "we started a workbook lesson on letter-copying. When the lesson was started, Roger came up to my desk and told me that Claude had stolen his ruler. He said his name was on it. I sent him back to his seat and quietly walked to where Claude was working. Yes, he was using the ruler. I took it from him and glanced at the back. There was Roger's name, just as you see it now on the ruler."

Mr. Trencher held up the ruler. It still said ROGER BEAM in blue Magic Marker.

Claude raised his hand, and Mr. Trencher looked at him. "Yes, Claude?" he said.

"So she hit me with the ruler, right on the hand—with *my* ruler!" Claude said. He felt tears come into his eyes again, just from thinking about it.

"Is that so, Mrs. Clipper?" asked Mr. Trencher.

"I felt he needed a lesson," said Mrs. Clipper. "We have too much stealing in this school."

"Too much stealing, yes," said Mr. Trencher, "and too much hitting."

Mrs. Clipper pressed her lips together and was quiet. She was tapping one foot on the floor.

For a moment nobody said anything.

Chapter 9

The Evidence about the Ruler

It was a long meeting and Claude began to feel tired. He also felt angry. He wanted to talk, to tell his part of the story, and nobody was letting him. He looked at his father, and his father smiled just a small smile and winked just a small wink. Nobody saw the smile and the wink but Claude. Suddenly he didn't feel so tired any more.

Then Mr. Trencher was speaking again. "All right," he said, "we have heard from Roger, and from Mrs. Clipper. Now let me ask a few questions. Claude?"

"Yes, Mr. Trencher?" said Claude.

"Is this your ruler?" asked Mr. Trencher, holding it up.

"Yes," said Claude.

"Where did you get it, Claude?" asked Mr. Trencher.

"My dad gave it to me, even when it wasn't my birthday," replied Claude.

"I see," said Mr. Trencher. "Mr. Sample, did you give this ruler to Claude?"

"Well, sir, I did give him a ruler just like that one. I gave it to him on Friday after supper. I taught him to measure with it."

"I see," said Mr. Trencher. "Well, I wonder whether there can be *two* rulers, just alike, one Claude's and one Roger's."

Claude was dying to say *no*, but his father said quickly, "I suppose there could be, Mr. Trencher. There were lots of rulers just like it in the store where I bought Claude's ruler."

Mr. Trencher turned to Claude. "All right, Claude, do you think there could be two rulers? Maybe you made a mistake."

"No," said Claude, "there's only *one* ruler, and it's mine."

"Then how did Roger get it?" asked Mr. Trencher.

"Well," said Claude, "when I went out to recess I left my ruler lying on my desk. Then—"

"That's right!" Otis interrupted loudly. "I remember he told me he left it on his desk and I told him that was a dumb thing to do."

"Wait, Otis," said Mr. Trencher. "We'll call on you if we need you. Go on, Claude."

"So I came back into Room 14 and my ruler was gone. My seat is right behind Roger's. Then Roger went up to the board to do that dumb letter-reading lesson—"

Mr. Trencher interrupted. "Stop, Claude. We're talking about the ruler, not about the lesson."

Mrs. Clipper started tapping her foot again. "My children all learn to write neatly," she said.

"We believe in neatness," said Mr. Trencher. "Now, go ahead, Claude, about the ruler."

"Roger went to the board," said Claude, "and I saw my ruler sticking out from under his notebook, so I took it back."

"But, Claude," said Mr. Trencher, "how did you know it was yours? It had Roger's name on it."

"I felt the notches," said Claude.

"Yeah!" Otis shouted. "A little, a little, a big, and a little!"

"Otis!" said Mr. Trencher. "We'll call on you when we need you." He looked at Claude. "What do you mean, the notches, Claude?"

"Feel on the '12' end of the ruler. You'll feel four notches," said Claude.

Mr. Trencher felt that end with his finger. "Yes, I feel them. I can see them now, too. What do the notches prove?"

Claude saw Otis raising his hand and bouncing up and down in his chair. "Otis can tell you," he said.

"All right, Otis, tell us," said Mr. Trencher.

"It was after Claude got the ruler," said Otis. "I was playing on his steps and he tried to write his name on the ruler, but it slipped off."

"Slipped off?" said Mr. Trencher.

"Yeah, it wouldn't stay on. The ruler was too shiny," said Otis. "The pencil wouldn't make much mark. Only a little. And Claude rubbed his thumb on the pencil mark and it rubbed off. I bet you could rub off Roger's Magic Marker name with your thumb."

Mr. Trencher looked at the ruler and rubbed the back with his thumb. "You're right," he said, "it rubs off." He held up the ruler and it now said OGER BEAM, and there was a blue smudge on Mr. Trencher's thumb.

"So Claude asked to borrow my knife—I always carry my knife—"

"In case of emergencies," said Claude.

"And I gave him the knife," Otis went on, "and he cut four notches, a little, a little, a big, and a little."

"Humph!" said Mrs. Clipper.

"Yes, Mrs. Clipper?" said Mr. Trencher.

"You see how they have practiced their story," she said. "They've made the whole thing up. They are always together. They are just making it up."

"That's possible," said Mr. Trencher. "But then how did the notches get on the ruler?"

"I don't know," said Mrs. Clipper. "Probably Claude cut them in the end when he took Roger's ruler from him, and then he and Otis made up the story."

"Roger," asked Mr. Trencher, "did your ruler have notches in the end?"

"I never looked," said Roger. "Maybe it did, but it has my name on it."

"But we can prove we cut the notches," said Claude. "We've got *evidence*!"

"All right, Claude, show us your evidence," said Mr. Trencher.

Claude leaned down beside his chair and opened his schoolbag. Everyone was looking at him. He felt around inside the bag and found the envelope. "Here!" he said, and he handed the envelope to Mr. Trencher.

Mr. Trencher looked closely at the envelope. Then he read aloud: " 'These four bits of wood found on step outside Samples' house on Monday afternoon. Found by Claude Sample, Otis Link, and Mr. and Mrs. Sample.' Did you write this, Mr. Sample?"

"Yes, I did," said Claude's father. "My wife didn't have time to sweep the steps." He smiled.

"Well, now, let's look at the evidence," said Mr. Trencher, and he carefully opened the envelope and tapped it until the four V-shaped pieces of wood fell on the glass top of the desk.

"Fit them! Fit them!" shouted Otis.

"That's just what I'm going to do," said Mr. Trencher. "Let's see: a little—*that* fits, a little—*that* fits, a big—*that* fits, and a little—and *that* fits!"

Mr. Trencher looked around at everyone. Then he said, "Claude, I think you have proved that this is your ruler."

"But," said Roger, "it has *my* name on it."

"All right, Roger, let me ask you a question. Do you have a blue Magic Marker in your desk?" said Mr. Trencher.

"I—I—I don't think so," said Roger.

"When did you write your name on this ruler?" asked Mr. Trencher.

"When I got it," said Roger.

"Just a minute," said Mr. Trencher. He pressed the buzzer on his desk. In a moment Miss Bell opened the door and came in.

"Miss Bell," said Mr. Trencher, "will you please go with Roger and help him look in his desk to see if there's a blue Magic Marker there?"

"Certainly, Mr. Trencher," she said. She smiled at Roger. "Come on, Roger, I'm sure we can find it if it's there." She took Roger's hand and they left the office.

Mr. Trencher looked around. He was about to speak when Mrs. Clipper said, "I was only trying to do my best." She looked at Claude. "Claude, I am sorry I said you were a thief. I see now that it was your ruler. I am also sorry I hit you. I thought you had stolen the ruler. But my evidence was not good. I—" and Mrs. Clipper—strict, firm Mrs. Clipper—looked down at her lap, and fumbled with her purse. She took out a handkerchief and wiped her eyes. She even sniffed.

Claude watched her amazed. He felt sorry for her. He looked at his father, but his father was looking out the window. He looked at Otis, and Otis was looking at Mrs. Clipper, with his mouth open.

Then Claude decided to say something.

"Mrs. Clipper?" he said.

She looked up but did not speak.

"Mrs. Clipper, I see why you thought it was Roger's ruler. After all, his name was on it, and I think you are right to be against stealing. I don't like it when my stuff gets stolen. I feel mad at Roger for stealing my ruler."

"Poor Roger," said Mrs. Clipper. "He doesn't have any friends. I don't think he knows how to make friends. He wants friends, and I try to be a friend to him. But he should not steal. Maybe he stole because he hasn't any friends. A friend would be much better than a ruler." Mrs. Clipper wiped her eyes again.

"Say, Otis," said Claude, "why couldn't we be friends with Roger? We—"

Just then Miss Bell and Roger came through the doorway into the office. Roger's eyes and cheeks were wet. He had been crying. He was holding Miss Bell's hand.

"Well," said Miss Bell, "Roger and I were able to find the Magic Marker. It's a blue one, all right." She turned to Roger. "Roger, tell them what you told me." She smiled and Roger sniffed.

"I don't know why I did it," he said. "I just saw the ruler on Claude's desk, and I wanted it, so I took it." He sniffed again. Tears were running down his cheeks. "I put my name on it with my Magic Marker. I thought that would fool everybody."

Mr. Trencher looked at Roger kindly. "Roger," he said, "what do you want most of all? A ruler?"

"I don't want a ruler at all," said Roger. "I want someone to play with."

"Hey, Roger!" said Otis. "Claude and I will be your friends. You can play with us."

"Aw, you don't want to be my friends," said Roger. "I stole Claude's ruler."

"Sure we do," said Claude. "And then, you can borrow the ruler whenever you want to—any time."

Claude's father cleared his throat. "Well, I've got to get back to work. Thank you, Mr. Trencher. Maybe everybody has learned something from this, right, Claude?"

"Right!" said Claude.

"What did you learn, Claude?" asked Mr. Trencher.

"Well," said Claude, "I guess I learned that the best thing there is, is to have friends." He stopped. "I also learned about evidence." He looked at Roger. "After school I'll show you how to measure things, Roger, if you want."

"O.K.," said Roger. He rubbed his nose.

"Good," said Mr. Trencher. He stood up. "I guess the meeting is over," he said. "Here's your ruler, Claude. I'm glad you and Otis and Roger are going to be friends."

"So am I," said Roger.

"Friendship is something you can't measure, even with a ruler," said Mrs. Clipper. "Now, boys, let's get back to Room 14."

"O.K.," said the boys.

The three boys walked out of the office together. As they went down the hall, Claude said, "After school I'll show you how to measure who has the biggest mouth."